W9-BNC-507

Copyright © 2019 Clavis Publishing Inc., New York

Originally published as *Zaza gaat slapen* in Belgium and Holland by Clavis Uitgeverig, Hasselt—Amsterdam, 2008
English translation from the Dutch by Clavis Publishing Inc., New York

Visit us on the Web at www.clavis-publishing.com.

Sweet Dreams, Zaza written and illustrated by Mylo Freeman

ISBN 978-1-60537-461-1

This book was printed in July 2019 at Wai Man Book Binding (China) Ltd.
Flat A, 9/F., Phase 1, Kwun Tong Industrial Centre, 472-484 Kwun Tong Road, Kwun Tong, Kowloon, H.K.

First Edition
10 9 8 7 6 5 4 3 2 1

MYLO FREEMAN

Sweet Dreams, Zaza

Clavis

NEW YORK

It is bedtime.

Zaza is almost ready to go to sleep.

But first, she wants to wish all her animal friends good night.

Zaza puts George Giraffe to bed.

George is so tall that he needs two beds!

Zaza pats him on the head.

"Good night, George."

Bobby is next.

Zaza gives her a tickle on the tummy.

"Sleep well, Bobby."

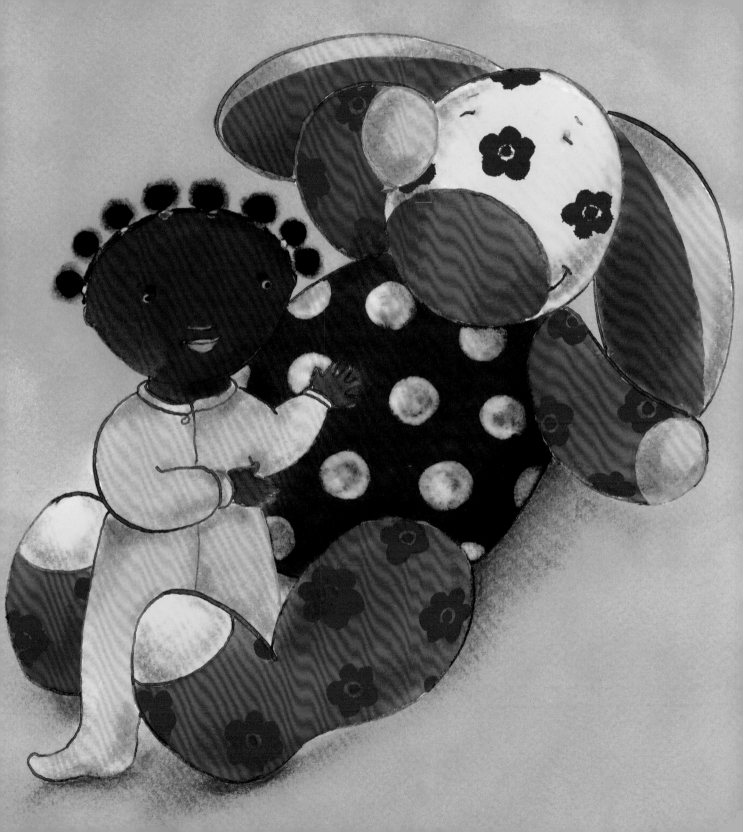

Zaza holds Mo and sings a lullaby for him.
"Rock-a-bye, Moey, in the tree top . . ."
Mo begins to fall asleep.

Pinkie gets a very soft cuddle from Zaza.
"Sweet dreams," Zaza whispers.

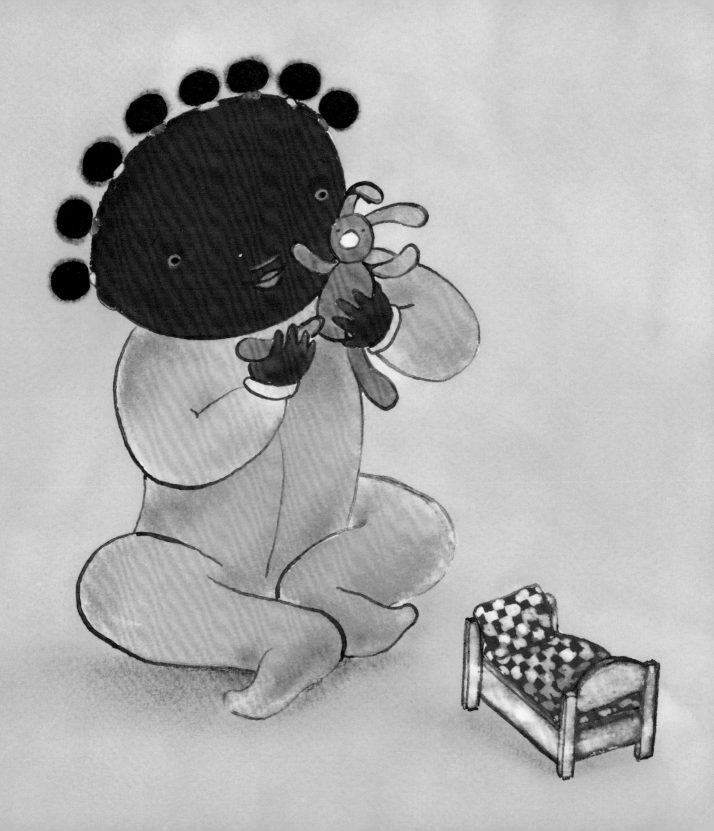

Now only Rosie is still awake.
Zaza loves all of her animal friends,
but Rosie is her favorite.
Zaza gives Rosie the sweetest kiss of all.

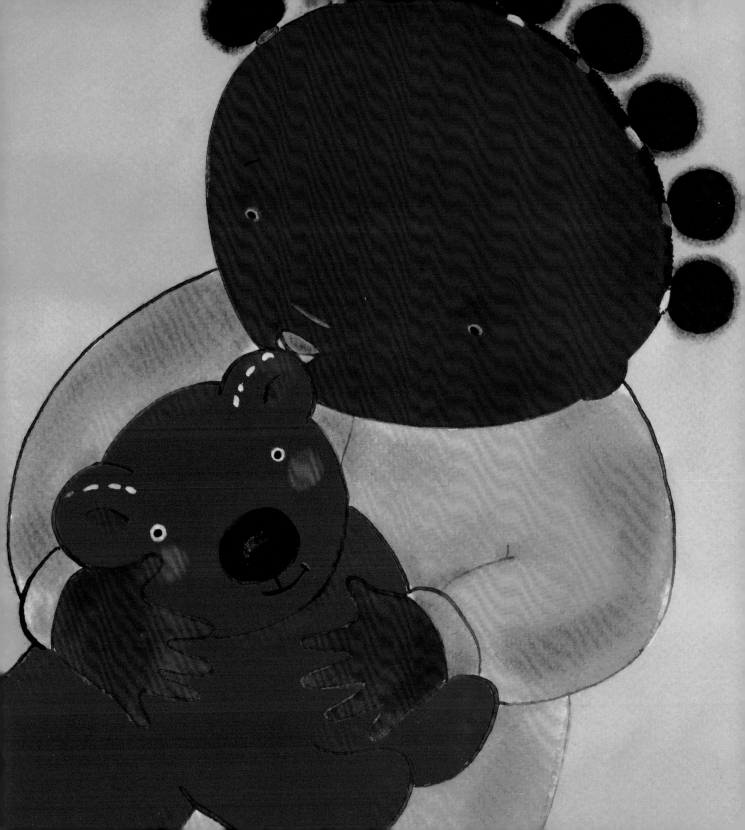

Then it is time for Zaza to go to sleep too.
Just like that?
No, first Mommy pats Zaza on the head.
She gives her a tickle on the tummy
and sings a lullaby.
Then Zaza gets a very soft cuddle and
the sweetest kiss of all.

Now Zaza can go to sleep.
Good night, Zaza.
Sweet dreams!